WHERE'S POLAR BEAR?

Nico Hercules

This book belongs to:

....

Polar Bear's gone
But where did he go?
He seems to have vanished
Somewhere in the snow.

He's got to be somewhere
But where could he be?
Perhaps he's gone snorkelling
By himself in the sea.

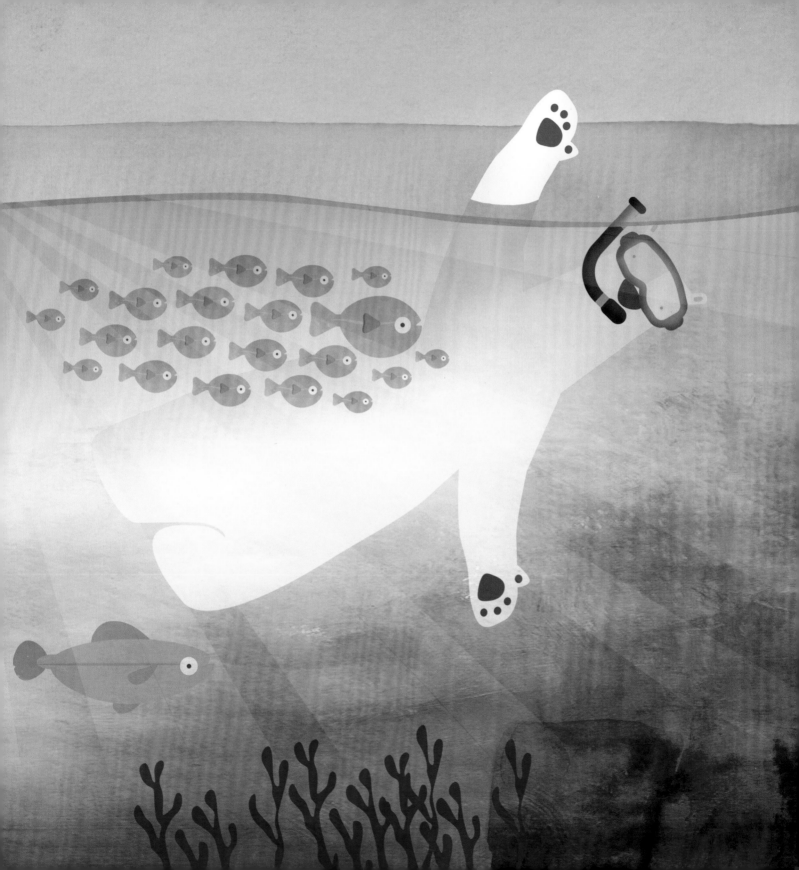

He could have been bored
And gone off for a stroll,
Or thought he'd go skiing
Across the North Pole.

NORTH POLE

He may have gone skating
With the grace of a swan,
Off into the distance
Until he was gone.

He might have gone curling
With a penguin or two,
Or paddled to France
In a handmade canoe.

Perhaps he went fishing
'Cause the weather was nice,
But fell down a hole
That he made in the ice.

He could have made plans
To go out for a meal,
With an interesting walrus
And a respectable seal.

RESERVED

Or went for a meeting
With a smart Arctic fox,
To have deep conversations
About the holes in his socks!

He may have gone shopping
To pick up some bits,
Like a new woolly sweater,
A scarf and some mitts...

...To put on a snowman
He's been building for hours...

...In a great igloo castle
With icicle towers.

But of course I'm just guessing
And I'm probably wrong,
'Cause there's more than a chance
He's been here all along...

Because nobody sees
Where Polar Bear goes
When he closes his eyes
And covers his nose...